VINYL DEMAND

VINYL DEMAND

Hayley Long

BBC

LARGE
PRINT

First published in 2008 by
Accent Press
This Large Print edition published
2009 by BBC Audiobooks by
arrangement with
Accent Press Ltd

ISBN 978 1 4056 2263 9

British Library Cataloguing in Publication Data available

Printed and bound in Great Britain by
CPI Antony Rowe, Chippenham and Eastbourne

Side One

1

Beth Roberts picked her post up from the floor. Flicking through the morning's delivery, she counted three pieces of junk mail, one skinny brown envelope which could only contain a demand for money, and a postcard from her parents in Spain. She pulled out the three pieces of junk mail and threw them on to a large and yellowing heap of similar envelopes in the corner of the hall, then made her way back upstairs to the flat.

In the rent book, 52c Queens Road, Cardiff, was described as a fully-furnished flat but really it was more of a poorly-equipped bedsit. It consisted of one large room which housed a single bed on each of the long walls and a small kitchen area in a corner at the far end. The only other objects which could count as furniture were an enormous old TV which looked as if it might be older than Beth and an even more massive music centre which was *definitely* a whole lot older than her and cased in polished wood. The music centre was only ever used as a coffee table because it was too old and useless to know what a CD was, let alone play one. Unframed posters of Justin Timberlake and Orlando Bloom clung to the walls and tried to cheer them up. Clothes lay scattered all over a scruffy dark-green carpet. The whole place was nothing more than a very shabby teen bedroom. Through a door across the hallway was a bathroom which was shared with the occupants of flats 52a and 52b. Beth Roberts didn't live in the best flat in Cardiff.

Beth flopped on her single bed and held the postcard up in front of her. It was the usual picture of a beach and sunshine. On the back her mum had written, *'Weather is here.*

Wish you were lovely!'

Beth sighed. Her parents had been living in Spain for almost three years now. They had moved there the week after she had taken her final GCSE exam and they had never really understood why she hadn't wanted to go with them. Looking around the bedsit, Beth couldn't really understand it either. But this was where her friends were and Cardiff was her city.

Beth fixed the postcard to the wall with some glue and then turned her attention to the envelope. Opening it, she saw that she was right. It was a bill. A gas bill. Printed in red ink was a demand for £76. A final demand. At the top of the bill in bold letters it said,

Failure to pay this bill within six weeks will result in your gas supply being cut.

Beth sat up. This was bad. No more

gas would mean no more meals of heated baked beans. No more noodles. No more boil-in-the-bag fish. No more bananas in custard. No more anything. No more gas would mean that Beth and her flatmate Rula would starve. And then what would she do? Write to her parents in Spain and ask them to rescue her? Tell them that she couldn't cope in Cardiff on her own?

Beth glued one corner of the red phone bill to the wall to stop it getting lost and got up from her bed. She crossed the room, pulled her mobile phone out of the pocket of a jacket which was hanging from a hook behind the door, and flipped it open. She pressed the speed-dial button and waited. Seconds later, a voice as young as Beth's but marked apart by a soft Polish accent answered.

'Hello?'

'Rula,' barked Beth into her phone. 'You haven't paid the gas bill.

I paid it last time, remember? You need to go to the post office and pay it.'

'Yes, I know.' There was a pause. 'I forgot.'

Beth gripped the phone a little tighter and rolled her eyes up to the ceiling. She and Rula had been best friends since they'd met in high school, way back at the beginning of Year 10. Back then, Rula had been painfully shy, homesick for Poland and hardly able to speak a word of English. But she'd had a fun twinkle in her eye and Beth had spotted that and decided that she was going to look after her. Sometimes, Beth felt as if she was still looking after Rula even now. Keeping her voice as calm as she could, Beth said, 'Well, you need to pay it now. It's seventy-six pounds, and unless you pay it quickly, we're going to get cut off.'

Rula's reply was cheerful and instant. 'I'll get it, Beth. I'll get it today and I'll get the bill and I'll pay it. Stop worrying. There are more important things in life to think about. See you later.'

And with that the call was over.

2

Rula Popek snapped her phone shut and slid it into the pocket of her jeans. She could tell that Beth was cross with her. It wasn't the first time and it surely wouldn't be the last but it still needed to be sorted out. Life was tough enough as it was.

Rula and Beth were always falling out. Sleeping in child-sized beds in a cramped bedsit wasn't easy. Not even when you were sharing with your very best friend. There just wasn't enough space and the only way to get any privacy was to go across the hall to the shared bathroom and lock the door. Rula had spent a lot of time sitting quietly on the edge of the bath just thinking about things and enjoying the fact that she was alone. And sometimes, when it all got too much, she would disappear for a few hours and walk through central

Cardiff looking into the shop windows at things she could never afford.

But they never fell out for long. Just as the lack of space and money pulled them apart, it also pushed them together. There was no room to sulk in 52c Queens Road. Sooner or later, one of them would open a couple of cans of beer and within minutes they'd be watching the ancient TV and laughing again. Even the lack of a sex life didn't really cause too much of a problem. 'I'm saving myself,' was Rula's promise, the day she hung her Catholic cross on the wall by her bed. Beth, with no cross above her bed, had smiled and said, 'As soon as I find a rich man with a nice flat, I'm out of here so fast you won't believe it.' But Beth hadn't found him yet and she didn't really seem all that fussed.

So for now, they were in it together. Two nineteen-year-old girls with crap jobs, no money, family in foreign places and no rich boyfriends with nice flats. They needed to stick together to survive.

Rula hurried down Cowbridge Road. She liked this street. It reminded her of the busy city streets back home in Poland. It was busy and noisy and full of interesting things to see and buy. To her left, a man shouted cheerfully at her, asking her to buy bananas from his fruit stall. She shook her head, smiled and walked on, almost bashing straight into another man who was pasting a large poster on to the side of a bus shelter. 'Easy love,' he said. 'Watch where you're going.'

Rula mouthed a 'sorry' and stepped to the side. As she walked on, she turned and glanced at the poster. It was a huge picture of a woman who looked barely any older than her or Beth. She had chocolate brown hair and a ring through her lower lip. Beneath her picture, in big capitals, were the words LISA

LASHES AT LIQUID. ONE
NIGHT ONLY!

Rula read the words and frowned.
It made no sense to her at all. Half of
the stuff she read in English made no
sense.

'Rula!' A shout made her turn.
There, on a bike, was Skunk.
Everybody knew Skunk and Skunk
knew everybody. Six foot four, black,
dreadlocked and almost always on
his mountain bike, Skunk was not an
easy man to miss. Nobody knew what
he did exactly but it seemed to
involve knowing everyone's name
and selling things. Rula smiled. 'OK,
Skunk?'

'Have one of these.' Skunk pushed
a piece of paper into Rula's hand.

Rula looked down at the flyer
which was already a little tatty from
being pressed between Skunk's palm
and his handlebars.

LISA LASHES

IS COMING AT YOU
LARGE IN LIQUID
COOL BEATS, BIG
BREAKS AND EVEN
LONGER LASHES . . .

NEXT THURSDAY

Rula frowned down at the flyer silently for a moment and then she read the words out loud to see if they would make any more sense. They didn't. Looking up at Skunk, she shrugged her shoulders and said, 'I've just read about this Lisa Lashes woman on a poster in the bus shelter. Who is she? And what does all this coming at you large stuff mean?'

Skunk sat back on his saddle and put his hands behind his head. 'Lisa Lashes is the best girl DJ ruling the decks in the world today. She's coming to Cardiff next Thursday. I can get you tickets if you want. Only twenty quid with that flyer.'

Rula crumpled the paper and pushed it into her pocket. 'No thanks. Right now, I've got to find seventy-six quid or our gas supply will be cut off and my flatmate will cut my head off. I can't afford twenty pounds to watch some girl play some boring old records.'

Skunk shook his head. 'You sure?

I'm not offering again.'

Rula continued walking up Cowbridge Road and shouted, 'I'm sure,' over her shoulder.

After a few minutes she came to a stop outside a window front which was almost entirely covered by the words POLSKA INTERNET. This was the internet café where Rula worked. It was owned by her Uncle Lado who had brought her with him from Poland four years earlier. She'd had other jobs since leaving school but all of them had involved working for people who had treated her a lot less softly than Uncle Lado did.

She pushed the door and went inside. The café was empty apart from Uncle Lado who was sitting behind a computer screen watching highlights from a Polish football match. He was a chubby little man with twinkly grey eyes and a grey beard to match. Without taking his eyes off the game, he said, 'Rula, what are you doing here? It's your day off.'

'Uncle Lado, I need to borrow some money.'

Lado looked up from the computer and sighed. 'Rula, Rula, Rula. I've got two children of my own. I can't keep putting my hand in my pocket every time you want to buy a new pair of trainers or a new CD. If you can't manage on what I pay you, get another job. Or live somewhere cheaper.'

Rula pulled a face. 'I can't live anywhere cheaper. I already live in the cheapest flat in the whole of Wales.'

Uncle Lado sighed again. 'What is it for this time?'

'The gas bill. If I don't have seventy-six pounds to pay the gas bill, they're going to cut off our supply and Beth is going to cut off my head.'

Uncle Lado laughed. 'It might do you some good. Teach you to be responsible.' He stood up from his chair and disappeared into the back room, calling out to her to wait. Rula sat down at one of the vacant computer screens and, having nothing better to do, typed 'Lisa Lashes' into the search engine. Seven hundred and twelve thousand hits came up on the screen. 'Wow!' said Rula to herself. 'She's popular.'

Uncle Lado reappeared holding an envelope. Rula forgot the computer screen and stood up. 'Seventy-six pounds,' said Uncle Lado, pushing the envelope into her hand. 'But it's not a gift, it's a loan, and I will take that money back from your wages whenever I want. You understand?'

'Yes. Thanks, Uncle Lado, you're the best.' Rula gave her uncle a delighted hug, pushed the envelope into her pocket and left.

*   *   *

Back on Cowbridge Road, Rula

breathed a huge sigh of relief and began walking home. Uncle Lado was right. She *did* need to manage her money better but it was hard to save anything when there was so little to save from. But then again, Beth managed to pay her share of the bills and it was hardly any easier for her. Beth worked at the other end of Cowbridge Road in an upmarket deli which sold Spanish sausage and green olives and tomato bread. Which all sounded very nice and lovely, except that the people in this part of Cardiff didn't actually want green olives and Spanish sausage. They wanted Clarke's pies and chips. The threat of being booted out of a job was always hanging over Beth's head.

Rula walked on, enjoying the sunshine and the noise and the life around her. In a window to her right, a woman appeared placing a new item on display. Rula spotted the movement from the corner of her eye and turned. A white Adidas tracksuit top with three red stripes running down the arms was being fitted over a plastic dummy. White and red. Like the Polish football team wore. Rula stopped to take a longer look. There was nothing else nice in the window. A yellowing wedding dress. A scruffy teddy bear. Some old books. The usual charity shop stuff.

Rula pushed open the door and went inside. The shop was busy. The charity shops on Cowbridge Road were always busy. Rula stood by the counter and waited while a woman in her fifties finished her long conversation with the volunteer shop assistant.

'It's terribly sad, isn't it? You don't expect to lose your husband at my age but life has to go on.'

'Of course it does, dear,' said the shop assistant, nodding sadly.

'And anyway, I haven't really got the room for all these.' The woman

19

stopped and pointed at three large boxes which were on the floor by her feet. 'I'll be looking for a smaller place to live and they do take up a lot of room. He loved his records, and some of these are probably worth a quid or two. People collect them, you know. But he'd have wanted them to go to a good cause.'

'Of course he would, dear,' said the shop assistant. 'Thank you very much for bringing them in.'

The woman turned away with a tearful smile and left the shop. In front of the counter Rula stood fixed to the spot, with her eyes on the boxes of records.

'Can I help you, dear?'

Rula looked up. She had been so lost in thought that she had almost forgotten where she was. 'Yes, please,' she answered. 'I'd like to know how much you want for those records.'

The shop assistant looked down at the boxes. 'Well, I don't know. The lady's only just left them here. Let's have a look, shall we?'

She came out from behind the counter and opened one of the boxes, flicking her fingers across the tops of the records. After a moment or two she stood up and shrugged. 'Well, the lady who brought them in reckoned they were worth a quid or two but it just looks like the usual old sixties and seventies rubbish to me. Nobody wants records any more. It's all CDs and MP3 players nowadays, isn't it?'

Rula nodded helpfully. 'Can I have a look, please?'

'Of course, dear.' The shop assistant returned to her side of the counter and began to serve the next person. Rula squatted down and pulled out one of the records from the box. It was called *The Very Best of Georgie Fame*. Rula had never heard of him, but he had a nice face and on the front of the record cover he was smoking a cigarette and looking very happy about life. She pulled the round black vinyl out from its inner sleeve and inspected it closely. She didn't know anything about vinyl records but this one looked alright. The black surface was shiny on both sides and it didn't appear to have a single scratch on it. She slid the record back into its sleeve and stood up again. The shop assistant had finished serving another customer and was free again. She nodded at Rula and said, 'Fifty pence each, love.'

Rula looked back down at the boxes. There had to be at least a hundred and fifty records there. 'How much for the whole lot?' she asked.

The shop assistant looked surprised. 'What, you want *all* of them? Well, in that case, how about fifty quid to take them all off my hands?'

Rula bit her lip, excited. She could afford that but she knew she was taking a big risk. But business was all about risk. There was no way she was ever going to make any money by being careful.

'Agreed!' Smiling, Rula dug Uncle Lado's money out of her pocket and counted off fifty pounds. 'I'll take one box with me now and come back for the other two. Is that OK?'

'Of course it is, love. Was there anything else?'

Rula was just about to say no when she remembered something else and laughed. 'Yes, there is, actually. How much do you want for that white and red Adidas top in the window?'

The shop assistant walked over to the window and took the tracksuit top off the dummy. She handed it to Rula with a smile. 'You can have that one for free, love. Seeing as how you've just taken all that junk off my hands.'

'Brilliant, thank you!' Rula tied the arms of the tracksuit top around her waist and lifted one of the boxes. It was very heavy. 'Good job I'm not going far,' she said, grinning.

Out on the street, Rula made her way home, struggling under the weight of the heavy box. But even though her arms ached and the box dug into her belly, Rula was feeling happy and excited. She had a plan for this little lot. She was going to take them all to her friend Jan who ran a second-hand music stall on Cardiff Market and turn her fifty pounds into a hundred pounds or a hundred and fifty pounds or perhaps even more. That way, she'd be able to pay the gas bill *and* get some decent food in *and* buy a few CDs *and* have enough money left for a big night out. There was no doubt about it, it was a great plan. Smiling to herself, she struggled on a little faster. She couldn't wait to tell Beth.

3

'YOU DIPPY TART!'

Rula took a deep breath and waited. She knew that Beth was not finished yet.

'YOU COMPLETE AND UTTER DIPPY POLISH TART!'

'Now that's just rude,' interrupted Rula with a frown. 'I'm proud to be Polish and I'm not a tart, thank you.'

Beth put her hands up to her head, gave it a frustrated shake and made a growling noise that might have contained the word 'sorry'. Then she said, 'Yes, but you *are* dippy.' With a sniff, she added, 'And stupid.'

For a moment, the two of them sat on their single beds in silence. Beth was staring moodily at the floor but Rula's eyes were still fixed on her boxes of records. When Beth began to speak again, it was in the slow, quiet voice of someone trying very,

very hard to keep calm. 'All I'm saying is,' she said between long, deep breaths, 'I find it very hard to accept that you have just spent the money for the gas bill on three boxes of clapped-out old rubbish.'

Rula looked hurt. 'It's not rubbish. People collect old stuff like this now. I got these all really cheap but we can make good money on them. Honestly, Beth, you have to trust me. My friend Jan has a record stall on the market and he'll give us a good price, I know he will. Even if he gives us just *one* pound for each record, it's still more than double what I paid for them.' Rula leaned back against her wall and smiled. 'Think what we could do with all that extra money. Not only would we pay the stupid gas bill but we could have some beers and a curry, get some new clothes, meet some blokes, go on holiday, get a flat down Cardiff Bay . . .'

Beth interrupted with a small smile. 'I think you'll find that we need to sell more than a few poxy old LPs before we can afford to move out of this dump.'

Rula pretended to be surprised. 'You mean that you want to live somewhere else? But, Beth, this is the *worst* flat in the whole of Wales. Actually, it's probably the worst flat in the whole of Britain. You should be proud to live here. One day they might turn it into a museum and charge people to come inside and have a look.'

Beth gave another smile which was still small but slightly bigger than the last one. 'Yes, well, it will be even worse if they cut the gas off, so you'd better be right about these records. Otherwise, there's going to be a serious falling out between Wales and Poland, let me tell you.'

Rula took out her phone and began pressing buttons. 'It will be OK, I promise you. Stop worrying. There are more important things in life to think about. I'll give Jan a call now and we'll sell the records as soon as we can. No point hanging about.' She waited a moment and then began to speak in the fast purring sounds of Polish.

Beth sat on her bed and listened. The noises sounded alien to her. Even though Beth had been Rula's best friend for four years, she had never picked up any Polish. Rula had once wanted to teach her some simple phrases to impress Uncle Lado and Aunt Magda but Beth had not been a good pupil. 'What's the point?' she'd argued. 'They can both speak English.' When Rula had said that it was just a matter of being polite, Beth had replied, 'Well, in that case, you lot should all be learning to speak some Welsh, shouldn't you?' It was Rula who had pointed out that Beth couldn't speak Welsh either.

Rula finished her call and beamed at Beth. 'Jan says we can take the records along now. I've told him the boxes are too heavy to carry all the way to town, but he says that if we take a selection he'll be able to get an idea of what he might pay us for the whole lot. You fancy a trip into town?'

'Of course,' said Beth, jumping up from her bed. 'I want to be rid of this rubbish as soon as possible. How are we going to carry them?'

Rula crossed over to the kitchen and took two large supermarket carrier bags from a cupboard under the sink. She handed one to Beth. 'Fit as many records as you can into this and we'll take one bag each.'

Beth looked at the carrier bag which Rula had handed her and shook her head in dismay. 'Not only have you blown the gas money on charity shop junk but you also expect me to walk into town carrying a Lidl bag. What if somebody sees me? It's too shameful.'

Rula sighed and shook her head. 'OK, *you* have the Tesco bag and I'll carry the Lidl bag. I don't care what people think.'

Minutes later, they were ready to go. As they locked the door of flat C, Beth spotted the white and red tracksuit top which was still tied around Rula's waist. 'A new Adidas top? Since when did you have the money to be buying Adidas?'

Rula turned around and grinned. 'I didn't buy it. The woman in the charity shop threw it in free with the records. Bargain eh?'

'Bargain,' muttered Beth as she struggled down the stairs of 52 Queens Road, with the Tesco bag bumping against her legs.

* * *

Rula's friend Jan sat on a folding camping-stool with the records spread out around his feet. Behind him, plastic crates filled with videos, CDs, DVDs and vinyl records were stacked at crazy angles on wooden shelves reaching high up into the roof of Cardiff's old market hall. From a small record-player on a table by his side, the rock music of Bon Jovi was blasting out and mingling with the sounds of the market. Beth looked him up and down with a wary eye. She was not surprised that Rula had never mentioned Jan before. He was a bit of an eyesore. He looked to be anything between twenty and thirty years old but carried the spare weight of someone who had been drinking large amounts of lager for much longer than that. A grey T-shirt which had once been black was stretched tightly over his bulging belly. On its front was printed the horns and skull of a goat and the word 'MEGADETH' in yellow, lightning letters. From his chin, a stiff ginger beard grew downwards in a straight line. His shaved head lay mostly hidden under a pale blue military cap apparently dating back to the American civil war. From one ear, a silver cross dangled against a ginger sideburn. When he spoke, it was with an accent which was a strange mix of Polish and Welsh.

'OK bud, let's have a look at what we've got here, then.' He picked up one of the records closest to him and inspected it. *'The Equals.* Great band. They blended sixties beat with a bit of the old reggae. Can't fault it.' Jan put the record down on the table and began to fill a pipe which had been lying on the shelf behind him. 'You know what? I played drums with a reggae band in Warsaw once. Those guys were mental. We played this one gig where the sound was all wrong and it turned out there was a dead body in the speaker. Can you believe that?'

Beth shrugged her shoulders and Rula smiled politely. Neither of them *did* believe it but they didn't want to upset the man who was going to buy their records.

Jan put the pipe into his mouth and picked up another record. '*The Mamas and Papas*. Groovy. See this big mama here?' He tapped a picture of a large, long-haired woman on the cover. 'Mama Cass. She sang like an angel but she partied like a hellcat. Made that Pete Doherty look like a pussy. Ended up choking on her sandwich.' Jan nodded thoughtfully to himself. 'Remember girls, *never* eat a sandwich when you're pissed. A sandwich can be a dangerous weapon in the hands of the pissed.'

'I'll try to remember that,' said Rula.

Jan placed the record on the table and reached down for another. Beth gave an inward groan. At this rate, they'd be here all day.

'Shirley Bassey!' Jan puffed happily on his pipe, sending out a cloud of blue smoke which made the two girls cough. 'Dame Shirley Bassey. They don't make singers like her any more. She's a living Welsh legend.'

'I've never heard of her,' said Rula.

'My nan likes her,' said Beth helpfully.

Jan looked up and gave Beth a look of admiration. 'You've got one damn groovy nana.'

Beth shrugged. 'She's a real sweetie but I wouldn't exactly call her groovy. No offence or anything, but nobody listens to the same rubbish as their grandparents, do they?'

Jan shook his head in amazement. 'Shirley's not rubbish! Have you never heard of this track "Spinning Wheel"? I tell you, it will blow your brains away. Play that in any club in Cardiff today and the dance floor will be packed.' He tapped another record with his toe. 'Curtis Mayfield. Play *anything* from this record and you'll have people hero-worshipping you.'

Beth picked up the Curtis Mayfield record and looked at it. On the front was a picture of a young black man wearing a very tight yellow suit. He looked quite good in it. She flipped the record over and began to read the names of the song titles on the back.

'Eight tracks of pure soul-funk genius,' said Jan, nodding at the record in Beth's hands. 'Only four songs on each side but every second you get is total top quality. Nowadays, bands have one or two killer tunes and fill up the rest of their albums with any old rubbish. It's all about quantity so that the record companies can charge a bit more. Nobody cares what it sounds like. But in the good old days of vinyl, you knew you were about to hear something great if there were a lean, mean four tracks on each side. Less is more. Remember that, girls.' Jan sat back on his camping-stool and stroked his beard thoughtfully. After a small pause, he nodded again at the record in Beth's hands and said, 'That album you're looking at is all killer, no filler.' And then he smiled, clearly pleased with himself.

Beth continued to examine the record cover and tried to ignore him.

'So how much?' said Rula, who was starting to look bored. 'I've got about a hundred more of these at home.'

Jan rubbed his hands together and thought for a moment. 'Tell you what. I'll give you twenty quid for the lot.'

'WHAT?' Rula and Beth stared at him, their mouths open with shock.

'Twenty quid. Take it or leave it.'

'I paid over double that to begin with,' said Rula, outraged. 'And you said these records are all really good.'

'Yes, but ladies . . .' said Jan, pulling at a tuft of beard, 'I have a business to run. And what's more, I've got hundreds of records to sell already.' He waved at the mountains of boxes behind him. 'I don't really need any more. I'm doing you a favour.'

Rula stared at him. Her face had gone a little green. 'Is twenty pounds the best you can offer?'

Jan pushed back his cap and scratched his head. 'Twenty-five. But that really is my last offer.'

Rula looked helpless. 'Oh God! If that really is the best you can do, then I suppose . . .'

Before she could finish, Beth interrupted. 'Rula, pick the records up. I've made a decision, we're taking them back home.'

Rula and Beth sat on the floor of 52c. All around them were records. Some were still in their sleeves and others were bare and black and gleaming a little in the light of the afternoon sun which shone in through the window. The records covered the floor so completely that not a single inch of the grotty green carpet could be seen. In the middle of the room, rising like an island among them, was the old, wooden music centre. Rula sat hunched up next to it with a big frown on her face. In her hands were a plug and a small screwdriver.

'Do you think you can fix it?' asked Beth.

'Of course,' said Rula. 'It just needs a new plug. I think that other one was older than Uncle Lado.'

Beth looked at Rula's frowning

face. 'If you can fix it, why do you look so worried?'

'I'm not worried,' snapped Rula. 'I'm just thinking. And anyway, there are more important things in life to worry about.'

'Yes, I know,' said Beth. 'You keep telling me.'

Rula screwed the plug back together and held it up for Beth to see. 'All done! Now for the moment of truth.'

She moved over to the wall behind her and pushed the plug into a socket next to Beth's bed.

'It's not working,' said Beth, disappointed.

Rula gave her a hard stare. 'That's because we need to switch it on, stupid.' She leaned over to the music centre and pressed a large square button clearly labelled with the word 'POWER'. For a moment nothing happened, then slowly an orange light began to grow in the middle of a dated display panel.

'It works!' shouted Beth. 'You've fixed it. I knew you had to be good at something.'

Rula picked up a record and threw it at Beth's head.

'Hey, be careful! That's the money for the gas bill you're throwing about,' said Beth with a glint in her eye. 'Now let's hear if these records really *are* any good.'

Beth picked up the Curtis Mayfield LP which Jan had spoken so highly of. The first track on side one was called 'Don't Worry, If There's a Hell Below, We're All Gonna Go'.

'It's not a very good title,' said Rula, reading over her shoulder. 'Not like "Sexyback".'

Beth snorted. 'You only think "Sexyback" is a good title because you fancy Justin Timberlake. I bet you don't even know what *Sexyback* means. At least Curtis Mayfield is trying to say something. In fact, it sounds like the kind of thing *you'd*

40

say. Let's hear it shall we?'

Beth pulled the record from its sleeve and placed it on the turntable. With a shaky hand, she lifted over the metal arm and put the needle down on the black vinyl. The old wooden speakers of the music centre crackled and popped. Beth frowned. Suddenly, the display panel burst into life with orange and green lights, and more sounds began to flood from the speakers. First, a heavy, electronic bass line filled the room. Then came the voice of a young American woman complaining about how people didn't read the Bible any more.

'She's right, you know,' said Rula. 'Nobody reads their Bibles any more.'

'This record is really weird,' said Beth.

Quickly, the woman's voice faded away and was replaced by that of a black American man. He was shouting through the speakers and telling everyone not to worry about what the woman had just said.

'When is the actual song going to start?' asked Rula.

'Shhh,' replied Beth.

After a moment or so, the man stopped shouting and gave a big scream. As his scream faded away, the music began, softly at first and then louder and louder. It was as if the speakers had suddenly come to life. The sounds of guitars, drums and trumpets filled every inch of the flat. And then came the voice. The man who had been shouting seconds earlier began to sing. His voice was high, effortless and very, very sexy.

Beth leaned back on her hands and nodded at Rula. *'That's* the start of the song.' She shook her head in wonder. 'And it's worth waiting for.'

Rula closed her eyes and listened. After a few minutes, she said, 'He sounds a bit like Justin Timberlake.'

Beth, still amazed, shook her head again. 'I hate to say it but he's better than Justin Timberlake. Much better.'

*   *   *

They sat on the floor and listened to the whole of the Curtis Mayfield album and when that finished, they sat and listened to the whole of the Mamas and Papas. When that finished, they found an album called *Talking Book* by Stevie Wonder and they listened to that, too. When that was close to finishing, Rula said, 'Do you think Stevie Wonder is his real name?'

Beth, who was by now lying on her back with her hands behind her head, smiled. 'Don't know. Don't care. He could be called Stevie Bollocks for all it matters. It still wouldn't change the fact that this record is totally amazing.'

Rula smiled. 'So you really like all this stuff, then?'

Beth gave a big grin. 'Never

43

thought I'd say it but this old crap is really cool. Not even the Black Eyed Peas match up to some of this lot.'

Rula put her head on one side, thoughtfully. 'Does that mean that you're not still cross about the gas bill money?'

Beth sat up, sharply. 'Shit! I'd actually forgotten about that for a moment.' She lifted the needle from the record, bringing the music of Stevie Wonder to an abrupt stop. 'It's not funny, Rula. We still *do* have to pay that stupid gas bill. Stevie Wonder and Curtis Mayfield can't heat our baked beans, however cool they are. We have to get that money somehow.' She rested her chin on her knees and frowned.

'Well, I didn't spend all of it,' said Rula with a hopeful smile. 'Look, there's still some of Uncle Lado's money left. Maybe the gas people will let us pay the bill a little at a time.'

She dug her hand into the pocket

of her jeans and pulled out the crumpled leftovers of Uncle Lado's seventy-six pounds. Two ten-pound notes, one fiver and a pound coin. Rula looked down at her hand. Screwed up with the notes was a piece of paper. She rested the money in her lap and smoothed out the paper so that she could read it. *Lisa Lashes is coming at you in Cardiff.* It was the flyer which Skunk had given to her earlier that day.

As Rula stared at it, an idea began to take shape inside her head. At first, it was small and uncertain but the longer she looked at the flyer, the clearer the idea became. It grew and grew inside her mind until, suddenly, she opened her mouth and shouted, 'Beth, this could be us!'

She held the flyer up in front of Beth. 'We can play records. We can be DJs. I can see it now. Flyers everywhere saying, "Coming at you large in Cardiff, your funky hostesses, DJs Popek and . . .

and . . ." '

'Mega Beth!' said Beth, her eyes shining. 'I'm gonna be DJ Mega Beth.'

She took the flyer from Rula's hands and glued it on to the wall. Stroking the flyer with her fingertips, she closed her eyes for a moment and dreamed. In her head, she could see flyers and posters covering every wall in Cardiff, and each poster had her name on it. Beth opened up her eyes and stared again at the crumpled piece of paper in front of her. 'Next time I stick a flyer up here, it's going to have DJs Popek and Mega Beth written on it.' She turned to Rula with a wide smile. 'You and me are going to be massive DJs just like this Lisa Lashes woman. We're going to take over the world.'

Side Two

1

DJs Popek and Mega Beth stood outside the King's Castle pub and looked up and down the busy street. They were feeling good. They were feeling special. A young woman approached, pushing her howling child in a buggy. As she drew level, she swore at them for taking up too much of the pavement and then continued on her way, still muttering and swearing. Seconds later, an elderly man staggered past, smelling of Special Brew. Pausing in front of them, he gobbed a brown ball of spit on to the pavement and then staggered onwards. Fat raindrops began to fall from the sky. DJs Popek and Mega Beth stopped feeling special and started feeling like ordinary Rula Popek and normal Beth Roberts again.

Beth looked anxiously at the sky

and then down at her watch. 'What time did he say he was coming?'

Rula folded her arms. 'Ten o'clock. He said he'd meet us outside the King's Castle at ten o'clock and he told us not to be late.'

Beth raised her eyebrows. 'That's a cheek! *He's* the one who's late. It's almost a quarter past. Give him another call and see where he is. I've got to be in work in half an hour.'

Rula pulled out her phone and was about to make a call when the loud parping of a bicycle horn caused her to stop and turn. With a squeal of brakes, Skunk pulled up on his mountain bike and greeted them with a big beaming smile.

'What time do you call this?' said Beth crossly. 'You said ten o'clock.'

Skunk looked at a huge watch on his wrist and shrugged. 'My clocks are always set to Skunk Time. It's less rigid than real time.' He swept his dreadlocks off his face and tied them into a fat ponytail before asking, 'Anyway, what can I be doing for you?'

'We need some record players,' said Rula. 'Two of them.'

'What?' Skunk looked confused. 'Say that again.'

'Record players,' said Beth. 'Can you get us a couple?'

Skunk looked at the two girls and frowned and then, slowly, a big smile crept over his face. 'Oh, you mean *decks*. You want some record decks.' He nodded to himself, still smiling. 'You can call them decks, turntables, battle-packs, magic circles, wheels of steel . . . Call them what you like but don't call them record players. Makes you sound like a couple of great grannies.'

'We'd like some decks,' said Beth.

'What sort?' asked Skunk.

Beth and Rula looked at each other. After a pause, Beth said, 'Ones that work.'

Skunk nodded. 'How much have you got to spend?'

Beth turned red and looked at the pavement. Rula smiled and said, 'Not much, actually.'

'How much?' asked Skunk.

Rula shrugged. 'About twenty-six pounds.'

Skunk threw his head back and laughed.

Beth said, 'We could pay a little more than that if you don't mind us paying you back weekly.'

Skunk scratched his chin. 'Give me your twenty-six quid up front and I'll see what I can do.'

Rula and Beth looked at him doubtfully.

Skunk sighed. 'I can't deliver if I haven't got any cash up front. Don't worry, you'll get it all back if I don't find anything.'

Rula paused for a moment and then dug the money out of her pocket and handed it to Skunk.

Skunk grinned. 'Good to do business with you, ladies. I'll speak to you very soon.' Then he flashed them an even bigger grin, hopped back on to his mountain bike and sped off up Cowbridge Road.

*   *   *

Rula was in the internet café when Skunk called. The street outside was being soaked by a summer shower and people were rushing by in search of shelter from the heavy rain. Every one of Uncle Lado's eight computers was being used and the café was filled with the sounds of clicking keyboards, low coughs and whirring printers. Seated behind a small desk in the corner of the room, Rula smiled to herself. She knew that Uncle Lado would be pleased. He liked the rainy Cardiff weather. It was good for business.

Rula poured herself a strong black coffee from a large tartan flask and cast a bored eye around the café. There was nobody interesting in today. There never was. Sometimes she liked to dream that a handsome stranger who looked like the double of Justin Timberlake would walk in and ask her for sixty minutes of internet time. 'Of course,' she'd reply and log him on to the computer closest to where she was sitting behind her desk with the master computer and the tartan flasks of tea and coffee. The handsome stranger would sit down and try to turn his attention to the World Wide Web but would be unable to keep his gaze from returning to Rula. By the time his hour was up, he and Rula would be deep in conversation, laughing like old friends and staring deeply into each other's eyes. Finally, he'd say, 'Come away with me. I don't own a computer but I do own a very large house. I want you to live in it with me.' Rula would nod and leave with him, knowing that her days of working in an internet café and saving herself for the right man were over forever.

But this never happened. She had once been invited to a game of bingo by Mike, a slightly shifty man in his fifties who had dyed his hair chestnut brown and came in every day to look at a website called *The Russian Roses Dating Agency* but she'd politely turned him down. The only other people who came in to use the computers were Uncle Lado's married friends from the Cardiff Polish Club, a group of Chinese girls who never spoke and several Welsh youths who tried to look at porn whenever they thought Rula wasn't looking.

Rula looked up and spotted flesh on a screen in the far corner. Sighing, she tapped a button on her master computer and the offending screen froze for a second and then went black.

'Oy! What did you do that for?' exclaimed a spotty boy in a baseball cap.

'You know why!' replied Rula.

The spotty boy grumbled, scraped back his chair and slouched off into the rain. Rula watched him go. Then she looked at her watch. She still had three more hours of her shift left to go. Three more boring hours. Slowly, she took a long deep breath and held it. Her record for holding her breath was one minute and twenty-one seconds. Maybe today she would beat it. She began to count silently in her head. Seconds in, her phone began to ring. She quickly let out her remaining breath, took a few deep gulps of air and picked up her phone.

'Hello?'

'Hi, it's Skunk. I've got you a pair of real beauties. Technics. They're the best turntables that you can get.'

Rula smiled. 'I don't care how technical they are, as long as they come with instructions.'

Skunk coughed. 'You won't need instructions. You'll soon pick it all up with a bit of practice. These have got to be the bargain of the century.

Thirty-six pounds and that includes a neat little mixer as well.'

'Mixer? What's one of them?' asked Rula.

From the other end of the phone, Skunk laughed. 'You won't get far without it. Being a DJ is a bit like being a top-notch chef. You're cooking up a recipe of great sounds to wow a hungry audience. You won't get far without a mixer. Thirty-six quid I said, didn't I? You can give me the other tenner when you can afford it. I'll bring them around to your flat this evening, yeah?'

'OK, thanks, Skunk.' Rula ended the call and then scrolled through her list of contacts for Beth's number. Any feeling of boredom had passed.

*   *   *

In Ellie's Deli at the other end of Cowbridge Road, Beth was counting cans of goose liver in the stockroom.

There were exactly thirty cans. Just as there had been exactly thirty cans last month. Nobody was buying them. Nobody was buying much of anything.

'How are we doing this month?' asked Ellie, the shop's owner, popping her head through the open door of the stockroom.

'Um, pretty good,' lied Beth. 'I think we've sold a bit more this month.'

Ellie, who had a lot of money but not much business sense, sighed with relief. 'That's good. I'd hate to let you go but I just don't know how long I can keep you on here if sales don't pick up. But maybe we're over the worst of it, eh?'

Beth nodded. 'I'm sure we are. And anyway, where else are people going to buy their goose liver and stuffed olives if they don't buy them from here?'

Ellie smiled. 'Exactly. We're the only shop around here providing these specialist food products. Word is bound to get around.'

Ellie disappeared into the shop leaving Beth on her own. Turning her back on the goose liver, Beth sighed and sank down on to the floor. Ellie had been expecting word to get around for the past two years but it hadn't yet. It was surely only a matter of time before she realised that the shop was a total loss and closed it. Beth's phone beeped. She plucked it from her pocket and saw that she had one new message. She pressed the 'OK' button and saw the words: 'SKUNK IS BRINGING RECORD PLAYERS TONIGHT!!!'

The words brought a smile to Beth's lips but only a very small one. Already the excitement of being DJ Mega Beth was wearing off. It was hard to feel excited about anything with no money, a terrible flat and days spent mostly counting cans of goose liver. Beth switched off her phone and gave a big sniff. An image of sunshine and sand floated into her head. With a sinking heart, she realised how much she missed having her parents around. Her grip tightened on her phone and she almost switched it back on to call them. All of a sudden, she wanted nothing more than to speak to them and beg them for a one-way ticket to Spain. It didn't matter that she didn't speak any Spanish and didn't have a single friend over there; she just wanted to be away from all of this. She would get a job as a barmaid or as a waitress or anything. She would make an effort and learn Spanish. She'd soon make some new friends. But then she remembered Rula's text message and, despite her gloom, she smiled again. Maybe things would get better.

2

Skunk lifted the record decks out of their battered boxes and placed them down gently on the green carpet. Using his sleeve, he rubbed at a dark sticky mark covering the power button of one of the turntables and then, pleased with his efforts, stood up. 'Technics. The Rolls-Royce of record decks. What do you think?' he asked.

Rula and Beth looked down at them. One deck had a perspex lid with a large crack running through the middle of it. The other deck had no lid at all. One deck had grimy, worn buttons which looked as if they'd been frequently soaked by the contents of spilled pint glasses. The other deck had buttons missing. Beth leaned forward to investigate a little closer. Both decks were held together with silver tape.

Beth straightened up. 'The Rolls-Royce of record decks? These look as though they should be towed away by the council!'

Skunk looked hurt. 'Well, they're not pretty but there's nothing wrong with them. These are the best you can get. You could drop a bomb on them and they'd still make your records sound sweet. Don't judge them by what they look like.'

Rula frowned. 'They do look like a big pile of crap, Skunk.'

Skunk shrugged and looked even more hurt. 'Well, they've been around. They've seen some action. Been pre-enjoyed.' He smiled and stroked the one cracked perspex lid. 'These babies have been to Ibiza and Cyprus and everywhere. The stories they could tell if only they could talk! Do you think a busy DJ like Lisa Lashes has brand new decks that look like they've never been played? Of course she doesn't. She sticks with the equipment she knows and trusts.' He patted the decks lovingly. 'These marks and scratches are badges of honour. You should be proud of them.'

Beth rolled her eyes. She knew that Skunk would defend the decks forever if she didn't shut him up. She decided to put him on the spot and hit him with the most important question of all. 'Do they actually work?'

Skunk pulled a shocked face. 'What kind of a man do you think I am? Do you honestly think I would take your money in return for something which *did not work*? Of course they work! You just need someone to set them up for you, that's all. I'd do it myself, only I'm very busy at the moment.' He looked at his watch and edged closer to the door. 'Anyway, I'd best be off. You can pay me back that other tenner whenever you have it.' He shook his head and muttered, *'Do they work?'* and then, with a wave of the hand, he opened the door and left.

'Shit!' said Rula. 'They don't work, do they?'

Beth bit her thumbnail and frowned down at their new record decks. 'They've *got* to work. We can't have been so stupid as to spend the gas bill money on a load of old LPs and two broken bloody record players. *Nobody* could be that stupid.'

Rula looked at Beth's scowling face and then back down at the decks. 'Maybe I can get them working,' she said, brightly. She scratched her head. She was good at changing plugs but that was about the limit of her electrical skills. The record decks stared back at her, battered and lifeless and covered in silver tape. Rula scratched her head again. This job looked as though it was more than just a matter of changing a plug. It looked like it needed a miracle.

Outside, from the street, came

three sharp blasts of a car horn. Beth walked over to the window and looked out. 'It's your Uncle Lado,' she said to Beth. 'Shall I throw my keys down?'

Rula nodded. Beth leaned out of the window and threw her flat keys down to Uncle Lado who was now out of his car and waiting, with cupped hands, on the pavement.

'We really need to get our door buzzer fixed,' said Rula.

Moments later, Uncle Lado appeared, carrying a large cake tin in his hands. 'Hello, girls,' he said with a cheery smile, 'I just thought I'd drop by to see how you are. I've brought you a baked cheesecake from Aunt Magda.'

He noticed the records and the turntables on the carpet and went quiet. 'What's this? Been buying some new toys?' Looking at Rula, he frowned and said, 'I thought you had no money!'

'They're mine,' said Beth quickly.

'I'm thinking of becoming a DJ.'

'And I am as well,' said Rula even more quickly. 'We're *both* going to be DJs but Beth bought all the stuff and she doesn't know how to set it up.'

Uncle Lado sank down on to his knees and a smile crept over his face. He ran a hand over the one cracked perspex lid and looked lovingly at the battered old turntable inside. 'Wow!' he said. 'I haven't seen a record player for years.'

'Decks!' said Rula. 'You can call them record decks, turntables, circles of magic or steel wheels but you shouldn't ever call them record players because it makes you sound like a great granny.'

Uncle Lado looked a little confused and gave a shrug. 'Well, whatever you call them, it's nice to see some records again. When I was a boy in Poland, we loved to get our hands on English and American pop music. These big old black LPs seemed like the most exciting things in the world. I can still remember the first time I listened to a record. It was at my friend Edek's house. He had just been given a record by Elton John. We thought it was the most amazing music we had ever heard.'

Behind his back, Rula and Beth exchanged a glance and tried not to laugh. Uncle Lado said, 'Shall we set them up, then?'

Rula and Beth immediately stopped sniggering at him and exchanged another glance. 'Can you get them working?' asked Beth.

Uncle Lado shrugged. 'I don't see why not. I just need to wire them up to an amp and some speakers. I can use the amp and speakers on your old music centre for now. The person you bought them from did say that they work, I hope?'

Beth and Rula looked at each other uneasily. 'He *did* say that, yes,' said Beth. 'I'm just not sure that I believe him.'

'Well, we'll see, shall we?' Uncle

Lado patted his many pockets and pulled a screwdriver out of one of them. Rula smiled. She had depended on Uncle Lado for six years. Ever since her mother had died. And Uncle Lado had never let her down once. She put her hand into the pocket of her jeans and crossed her fingers.

*   *   *

Ten minutes later, Rula uncrossed her fingers and began to dance. The voice of Curtis Mayfield was loudly filling the room. A huge, glowing smile was covering Beth's face. 'They work!' said Beth in disbelief. 'Skunk was telling the truth! How completely brilliant is that?'

Rula laughed and danced around and around on the green carpet, carefully avoiding the LPs which lay littered across the floor. She danced over to Uncle Lado and, giving him a tight hug, said, 'Uncle Lado, you are the best uncle in the world. Do you know that?'

Underneath his beard, Uncle Lado smiled and went a little red and then grumbled, 'I don't like this music you're playing. It's rubbish. Have you got any Elton John?'

Rula and Beth roared with laughter and pushed the volume control up to maximum so that Curtis Mayfield was as loud as he could possibly get. From the flat next door, the sound of angry knocking rattled the thin walls. Uncle Lado shook his head, grumbled a little more and went home.

*　　　　　*　　　　　*

Three hours later, Uncle Lado was back. This time, instead of a cheesecake, he was carrying a small bundle of records. Beth threw the keys out of the window so he could let himself in.

Uncle Lado climbed the stairs

three at a time and rushed to the door of 52c, which was already open in preparation for his arrival.

'Two visits in one day!' said Rula. 'Visit us much more and we're going to have to start charging you rent.'

'I've bought you some more records,' said Uncle Lado with a smile. 'Good ones!'

Rula and Beth took the records from him. There were five of them.

Love Songs by Elton John
Music of the Polish Marching Bands
Polish Folk Songs
TV Hits of the 1970s
Push by Bros

'Thanks, Lado,' said Beth. 'This will have the people of Cardiff really packing the dance floors.'

Uncle Lado nodded and smiled. 'Yes, yes, that's what I thought. You've got something for everyone in that little lot. From timeless classics to . . .' He nodded at the Bros album,

'. . . young trendy stuff.'

Beth bit her lip and looked at the cover of the Bros album. It was covered in pictures of three pouting boys with Pat Butcher haircuts and carefully ripped denim. In tiny print on the back cover, a date told her that this record was exactly one year older than she was. Beth bit her lip again and then said, '*Very* young and trendy, thanks ever so much.'

Uncle Lado beamed back, pleased. 'So have you two girls been practising?'

Beth and Rula looked at each other.

Uncle Lado sighed. 'You want to be DJs, don't you?'

The girls nodded.

'So you need to practise and practise and practise. Do you think Fat Boy Thin grew to be such a big successful DJ by sitting around doing nothing? Of course not! He practised and practised and practised and that's what you need to start doing right now.'

This time it was Rula's turn to bite her lip and hide her smile. 'Fat Boy Thin? Uncle Lado, I never knew you were so up-to-date with your knowledge of the club scene.'

'Yes, well . . .' said Uncle Lado, looking pleased again. 'I like to know what's going on in the world.' He scratched his beard thoughtfully. 'And I also like the fact that you two have finally hit upon a good idea and shown a bit of ambition for once.' He paused for a moment before adding, 'Which is why I have decided to be your manager.'

Rula and Beth looked at him in astonishment.

'Umm, I don't think we need a manager yet, Uncle Lado,' said Rula.

Uncle Lado gave them a hard stare. 'Do you have any bookings?' he asked.

The two girls shrugged. 'We were going to worry about all that later,' said Beth.

Uncle Lado smiled. 'I don't want you to worry. I want you to practise. Learn to play those records so smoothly that I can't hear any gaps. You do that. I'll do the worrying. Agreed?'

Rula and Beth looked at each other, smiled and shrugged.

'Agreed,' they said.

Uncle Lado gave another smile. 'Good! Because I've already got you your first booking. Next Thursday evening, so you'd better get practising like I said.'

Rula and Beth stared at him, their eyes round with surprise and excitement. 'You've already got us a booking!' said Rula. 'Where?'

'Is it Liquid?' asked Beth. 'Or is it Jumping Jacks? Or Clwb Ifor? Or Eternity? Where is it?'

'It's even better than that,' said Uncle Lado, his smile breaking into a big toothy grin. 'You need to polish up your DJ skills because I've booked you to play at a Young

Farmers' Social Event at the Jolly Chef service-station in Builth Wells. It's going to be totally crazy.'

3

'Are we nearly there yet?' asked Rula, her eyes fixed on the road ahead of them. 'I feel sick.'

'It's just another few miles,' answered Uncle Lado. He twisted in the driving seat and turned to check on his niece who was sat hunched up and miserable on the back seat of his Skoda Fabia estate. Next to him, Skunk shrieked and grabbed hold of the steering wheel. 'Watch it, man! Will you STOP turning around to talk to the girls and keep your eyes on the road, please? You're gonna give me a heart attack in a minute.'

'Sorry,' said Uncle Lado and turned his attention back to the winding road ahead. All around them, pine trees covered the sharply sloping hills as they purred along the narrow road which cut through the heart of the Welsh countryside. On the back seat of the car, next to Rula, Beth watched the scenery unfold from her window. It was a long time since she had travelled north of Cardiff and the dramatic change of landscape amazed her. Wales was beautiful. She smiled to herself. Surely her parents' adopted Spanish home of Salou could not match this?

'What did you say this place was called again?' grumbled Rula.

'Builth Wells,' said Uncle Lado. 'It's not too far away now.'

'*Bwilf Wells*?' muttered Rula. 'I've never even heard of it. Why would anyone want to have a party out here?'

Uncle Lado turned around. 'It's in the very middle of Wales, so it's an equal distance for people to travel wherever they are coming from.'

'KEEP YOUR EYES ON THE ROAD!' screamed Skunk.

Uncle Lado apologised and stared quietly at the road ahead. Skunk gave a deep sigh. He was beginning

76

to regret his offer to act as a roadie. Uncle Lado's driving was too terrifying. Next time—if there *was* a next time—he would ask for danger money.

Outside, the trees began to thicken and the road plunged downwards into a natural valley. Near the road's edge, a grey stone cottage crouched beneath the trees and breathed out a thin white wisp of smoke from its chimney. It was the first sign of life they had seen for several miles. Uncle Lado steered the Skoda around a sharp bend. A whole row of grey stone cottages greeted them. All had thin wisps of white smoke rising straight upwards from their chimneys even though it was the middle of summer. The Skoda rounded yet another corner and there, in front of them, was the town of Builth Wells.

'You can stop feeling sick now,' said Uncle Lado to Rula. 'We're here.'

It didn't look like a very big town.

Beth glimpsed a small, pretty high street directly ahead of them before the car made a sharp right turn and crossed a bridge over a narrow, fast-running river. Beth peered curiously out of the car window. It was certainly a very pretty little town. It looked like a nice place to come for a picnic. It didn't really look like the kind of place to come for a party, though.

'Do you think anyone is actually going to turn up to hear us play?' she asked.

'Oh, there will be plenty of people there,' replied Uncle Lado. 'My friend Henryk knows a lot of these Welsh farmers. He trades in cheap tractor spares from Eastern Europe. He says that compared to the Polish, these Welsh are a bit socially backward but they're still more fun than the Ukrainians and the Russians.'

In the back, Beth gave a loud sniff. 'Er . . . you may have forgotten but I

78

am *still* Welsh, Lado.' She sat back in her seat and folded her arms crossly. 'And so is Skunk, so be careful what you're saying.'

From the front seat, Skunk shrugged his shoulders. 'Don't bring me into any national debate. I'm a citizen of Planet Earth, me.'

Uncle Lado laughed. 'Yes, we are *all* citizens of Planet Earth. It's just that some of us know how to enjoy ourselves more than others.' He took another right turn and came to a stop in a small gravel car park. 'Here we are! Your venue for your first booking as professional disc jockeys! The start of something wonderful!'

* * *

The Jolly Chef at Builth Wells did not look like the start of anything wonderful. It stood sandwiched between a petrol station and a Burger King and had large posters of fried breakfasts filling almost every window. On a chalk board outside, somebody had written

here tonight from 7.30 pm
Young Farmers'
Disco
With DJs Popek
and Mega Bath

'You see?' said Uncle Lado pointing at the board. 'You already have your name up in lights. Tonight Builth Wells. Tomorrow the World.'

'They've spelt my name wrong,' snorted Beth.

Between deep gulps of fresh air, a sick Rula tried to hold in a giggle. 'At least it makes you sound like a very *clean* DJ.'

Beth sighed and got out of the car. Skunk was already bent over the Skoda's open tailgate and coiling long lengths of speaker cable around his arms. 'Take these and stop moaning,' he said to Beth and passed her two Lidl carrier bags packed full of records. 'You need to start smiling. If those Technics turntables pick up your bad energy, they'll stop working.'

Beth scowled at him, took the records and walked into the Jolly Chef. Heads turned to look at her as she pushed open the doors. Beth paused. All around her, people were tucking into plates of omelette and chips and drinking tea from large mugs. The café was still open for business. There didn't seem to be any sign of a party crowd.

Uncle Lado hurried through the door behind her and began to talk quickly in Polish to a man who had appeared out of the kitchen wearing chef's whites. After a few minutes of fast Polish conversation and much laughter and back-slapping, he turned to Beth and said, 'Henryk says we should set up in the corner. That way, we won't be blocking the route out to the toilets.'

Beth frowned. 'That was Henryk?

I thought you said he was a trader in Eastern European tractor parts?'

Uncle Lado nodded. 'Oh yes, he is. But he has two jobs. Keeps his hands in lots of pies.'

Beth shrugged and turned to help Skunk who had just appeared through the door carrying twice his own bodyweight in electrical equipment. He spotted Beth's frown and said, 'I thought I told you to start smiling, girl. You've got a face like a funeral and Rula is still outside trying not to puke. Some opening gig this will be!' He turned to Uncle Lado and, nodding at the people still eating, asked, 'When are they kicking this lot out?'

'Oh no,' said Uncle Lado cheerfully. 'The café will stay open and the Young Farmers will party around them. It would be silly to turn away any business. This is the only service-station for miles and miles.'

'Great!' muttered Beth. 'This is getting better and better. We're

82

going to be playing Curtis Mayfield and Stevie Wonder to an audience of people more interested in eating their baked beans!'

Skunk put a hand on her shoulder. 'Look, girl,' he said sternly. 'It might not be Liquid and it might not be Eternity but it's your first gig and you've got to take whatever comes your way. You don't know who might pass by and hear you play. You've got to treat each and every gig like it's the most important gig of your life.'

Beth sighed. 'OK, whatever you say, Skunk.'

Behind them Rula appeared, wearing her charity-shop tracksuit top. She was still looking slightly green but had a smile on her face. In her arms, she was carrying more records.

'I've been thinking,' she said. 'I reckon we should start with the "Theme to Mission Impossible" and then blend it into Curtis Mayfield's "Don't Worry" and then follow on with "Spinning Wheel" by Shirley Bassey. I think that would be quite a funky way to start things off. What do you reckon?'

Finally, Beth smiled. So what if the Jolly Chef in Builth Wells wasn't the most glamorous venue for their first DJ experience? Suddenly it didn't matter. They had spent over twenty hours practising and that was almost a whole day. They now knew how to blend one record into another without a gap or a jolt or a clash of beats even if their improved skills had come at some cost. Georgie Fame now had a bad scratch on his opening track and they'd had a nasty row with their neighbours about the noise levels. But these were small prices to pay in the pursuit of DJ perfection. So what if the venue was wrong? Beth knew that their records would sound great wherever they were played.

4

The Jolly Chef was getting busy. Among the first to arrive was a minibus filled with farming students from Bangor University. Clearly their party had started some time before their journey down from north Wales had begun. One of them, a young man with a perm and warts, staggered over to where Rula and Beth were doing their soundcheck and watched, a sneer growing on his lips.

'Is this lot all yours?' he said, nodding his head at the turntables and records.

Rula and Beth nodded.

Wart-Face laughed. 'No,' he said and took a swig from a can of beer. 'No, can't be. Girls don't play records.'

'These ones do,' said Beth, without a smile.

'No,' said Wart-Face, shaking his head. 'No, I don't believe it. You're just borrowing this stuff from your brother or something.' He took another swig from his can and gave a loud burp. 'Can I have a go? I've always fancied myself as a bit of beat master, if you know what I mean. Here, let me have a go.'

He put his beer can down on a pile of records and tried to push his way past Beth to get behind the decks.

Beth shrieked, 'GET THAT BEER CAN OFF MY VINYL!'

Wart-Face looked at her in surprise. 'OK, OK, there's no need to . . .'

'GET THAT BEER CAN OFF MY VINYL AND GO AWAY.' Beth took a couple of deep breaths to control herself and then said calmly, 'Touch my records and I will kill you. I seriously mean that.'

'Touch *our* records,' corrected Rula. 'Touch *our* records and she will kill you.'

86

'Alright!' said Wart-Face, turning pale. 'Alright, alright! Point taken.' He picked up his can and turned to move away but before he left, he said, 'I can tell you now, ladies, neither of you will be leaving here on *my* arm tonight. You've just blown your chances right out of the water.'

Beth and Rula looked at each other and then back at him. 'We'll cope,' said Rula with a shrug.

Wart-Face staggered off towards the opposite corner where Henryk was arranging cans of beer and cider on a makeshift bar.

Rula and Beth turned their attention back to sound-checking their records and treated the room to a short burst of Shirley Bassey.

From a table close by, a young woman pushed her half-eaten all-day-breakfast away from her and stood up. She walked over to where Rula and Beth stood behind their record decks and greeted them with a 'Hi' and a cheery smile. Only Beth returned the smile. Rula was bent over one of the turntables with headphones covering her ears and was, for a moment, unaware of the world around her.

'I like this tune you're playing,' said the young woman. 'What is it?'

'"Spinning Wheel" by Shirley Bassey,' replied Beth.

'Shirley Bassey? Cool! What a great idea! I'd never have thought of playing any of her stuff but it sounds really great. Mind if I have a look at what other records you've got there?'

Beth gave her a wary look. She seemed OK. She was dressed in scruffy jeans and a hoodie but they were the sort of scruffy jeans and hoodie which looked like they cost an awful lot of money. They certainly didn't look as if they'd been found in any charity shop on Cowbridge Road. Through her lower lip was a gleaming silver ring. That looked expensive too. The woman didn't look as though she needed to steal any records from anyone.

Beth shrugged. 'Sure, why not?'

'Cheers.' The woman grinned. 'I promise you I won't mess any of it up. You won't need to kill me or anything.'

Beth turned red. 'Oh, you heard that? No offence but your mate seemed like a total arse.'

The woman pulled a face. 'He's not my mate. Do I look like a young farmer? I'm just travelling down to a club in Cardiff with my friends. This is the first service-station we've found for miles.'

She lowered her eyes and began to flick through the pile of LPs on the table. Beth smiled to herself. This woman, with her pierced lip and expensive hoodie, really *didn't* look like a young farmer. And now Beth came to think of it, her accent was from the Midlands and definitely not from any part of Wales at all.

The woman put the records down and straightened up. 'You've got some really good stuff here. Keep on collecting it.'

From behind, someone shouted, 'Lisa, are you coming? We've got to be at Liquid by ten.'

The young woman rolled her eyes. 'Got to go. Bye.' She waved at Beth and then turned and disappeared with her crowd of equally cool and expensively-dressed friends.

Beth watched her go and scratched her head. Something about the woman had rung a bell inside her mind but she couldn't think why. Next to her, Rula pulled her headphones off her ears and said, 'I think we've got all the volume levels just right now. I think we're ready to start.'

Beth gave her an excited look. 'Shall I put the first record on or do you want to do it?'

'You can,' said Rula with a grin.

Beth took the soundtrack to *Mission Impossible* out of its sleeve and put the black vinyl record on to

90

one of the turntables. Then, with a shaking right hand, she lifted the needle and placed it down on to track one. With her left hand, she slid the volume controls up to maximum. The speakers of the Jolly Chef thundered into life. The party had started.

*   *   *

Rula and Beth were having a seriously good time. All thoughts of their crap flat and crap jobs were temporarily forgotten. Playing fantastic records at maximum volume was a great way to pass the time even if it was inside a Jolly Chef roadside café. Beth couldn't remember when she had last had quite so much fun. She even started to moonwalk behind her decks.

Sixty young Welsh farmers and several happy motorists were jumping up and down to Herbie Hancock, when Skunk came hurrying into the café. Having helped to set up the equipment, he had disappeared outside for a 'special' cigarette and had not been seen inside the Jolly Chef for some time. He pushed his way through the crowd of jumping farmers and made his way over to Rula and Beth.

'Guess who I've just been talking to?' he shouted above the noise of the speakers.

'Michael Jackson,' said Beth.

'The Pope,' said Rula.

'No, no,' said Skunk, a big smile on his face. 'Not bad guesses, though. Try again.'

Beth puffed out her cheeks and thought hard. 'Gary Barlow?'

Skunk shook his head and looked at Rula.

Rula shrugged. 'Prince Harry?'

'No.' Skunk grinned and paused for effect. 'I have just spent the last half an hour outside in the car-park talking to *Lisa Lashes*.'

Rula and Beth stared at him. The

Herbie Hancock record began to fade. Quickly, Beth jumped into action and blended it into 'Uptight' by Stevie Wonder. The young farmers cheered happily.

'Lisa Lashes? Here? You are joking?' said Rula.

Skunk shook his head.

'What would Lisa Lashes be doing in the Jolly Chef at Builth Wells?'

Skunk grinned. 'Lisa and her crew stopped off here on their way down to Cardiff. Last night, they were playing at the *Dance by the Sea* festival in Rhyl. They're on their way to Liquid now. I told them that I'd be there myself if I wasn't here helping you lot.' He paused and took a large spanner out of the pocket of his trousers. 'This spanner undid the wheel nuts on Lisa's van.'

Rula and Beth looked at him, confused.

Skunk explained, 'They were running late as it was but then they got outside and found they had a flat tyre.' He smiled and looked proudly at his spanner. 'I helped them to change it,' he said.

Beth stared at him and in her mind a bell began to ring louder and louder until, finally, she said, 'OH MY GOD!'

Skunk and Rula looked at her.

'I SPOKE TO HER!' said Beth. 'I *spoke* to Lisa Lashes. She was right here chatting to me and I thought she might be trying to nick our records. I even thought she was a young farmer at first. But it was *Lisa Lashes* . . .'

Beth went silent for a moment and stared in wonder at the pile of records on the table next to her. Shaking her head in amazement, she added, 'She said she really liked the Shirley Bassey record we were playing. She said playing Shirley Bassey was a great idea. OH MY GOD!'

'Hang on a minute,' said Rula. 'If you saw her, why didn't I see her?'

'You had the headphones on and were looking the other way,' replied Beth.

'Typical!' muttered Rula.

'You know what this means?' said Skunk, excited.

Rula and Beth shook their heads.

'It means that you can say you were discovered by Lisa Lashes on your very first gig. That's bound to get you some more bookings. Tonight Builth Wells, tomorrow Ibiza.'

From out of the crowd, Uncle Lado appeared. 'Tomorrow Magor Services,' he said, cutting in on the end of the conversation.

'What?' Rula, Beth and Skunk turned to look at him.

'Tomorrow Magor Services. I've got you another booking. This time you'll be playing at a party at the Light Bite Snack-Stop at Magor Services.' He looked at their blank faces and then added helpfully, 'It's on the Welsh side of the

Severn Bridge.'

Before anyone could reply, they were joined by Henryk. He had a can of beer in one hand and a wad of ten-pound notes in the other. On his face was a beaming smile. 'This lot love you,' he boomed. 'They are really digging your funky music. I am very happy,' he said. 'Very happy.'

Beth and Rula smiled.

'Well, that's always nice to hear,' said Beth.

Henryk emptied the contents of his can of beer down his throat, crushed it and threw it over his shoulder, narrowly missing the head of Wart-Face who was jumping around behind him. 'I want to pay you now in case I am too drunk later,' he said. He pressed the wad of ten-pound notes into Beth's hand and added, 'Two hundred pounds. Thank you.'

Beth looked down at the money in her hands. She had never held two hundred pounds before. It felt nice.

Before she could get used to the feeling, Uncle Lado took the money off her and began to shuffle through it.

'I'm just taking back the seventy-six pounds that Rula owes me.' He looked at his niece and winked. 'But I'm a kind man so I'll call it seventy.'

He counted out seven ten-pound notes but, instead of stopping, he carried on to ten. 'Plus I'm adding thirty pounds to cover my fee as your manager. That makes a nice round figure of one hundred pounds.'

He looked up and saw the girls' outraged faces. 'I think that is a very reasonable fee,' he said with a shrug.

Beth put out her hand to take back the remaining hundred pounds but Uncle Lado held it back from her.

'Plus,' he added, 'I need thirty pounds to cover the cost of petrol and fifty pounds to pay Skunk for his help this evening.'

He peeled off five ten-pound notes and passed them to Skunk, who accepted them with a grin. Uncle Lado folded up one hundred and thirty pounds and put it into the pocket of his shirt.

'And this is for you,' he said, finally. He passed one ten-pound note to Rula and one ten-pound note to Beth.

'TEN POUNDS!' said Beth with an outraged laugh. 'Are you serious?'

Uncle Lado shrugged again. 'There are always hidden costs at the beginning of any new business venture but you'll earn more next time.' He smiled. 'And at this rate, you'll soon be raking in the money. Trust me.'

Rula snorted. Beth gave another outraged laugh.

'So,' said Uncle Lado. 'Tomorrow at Magor Services. Are you interested?'

Rula and Beth looked at each other and then at the ten-pound notes in their hands.

'We still don't have the money for

the gas bill,' said Rula. 'What do you reckon, DJ sister?'

Beth looked at the jumping farmers in front of her. Then she looked down at the records stacked in piles next to the battered turntables. A feeling of warmth welled up inside her and her mouth curved into a wide smile.

'You know what?' she said to Rula. 'I reckon that there are more important things in life to worry about than gas bills. I say we keep on spinning those wheels, sister!'